Mystical Way of Time

Mystical Way of Time

By
Kurt W. Oster, LCSW, RPT™

All Genders Press
www.allgenderspress.ca

an imprint of
Perceptions Press
Victoria, BC
Canada

2023

Mystical Way of Time

Published in 2023 by All Genders Press

Cover Illustration and Design: Margot Wilson
Illustrations: Margot Wilson

ISBN: 978-1-998924-59-2 (Paperback)
ISBN: 978-1-998924-60-8 (Kindle e-book)
ISBN: 978-1-998924-61-5 (Smashwords/Draft2Digital e-book)

Published in Canada by
All Genders Press
www.allgenderspress.ca

an imprint of
Perceptions Press
www.perceptionspress.ca
Victoria BC
Canada

Praise for Mystical Way of Time

Mystical Way of Time by Kurt Oster is a breath of fresh air among children's books as it invites a child to step into a wonderful world where everyone is celebrated just as they are. The illustrations and the words beautifully beckon and welcome the reader to engage in the magic of their imagination and join a cast of characters along a journey that lifts all of the restrictions of the mundane world. Celebrating and affirming the uniqueness of every person, this book is sure to be a rich source of encouragement and empowerment for every child while providing a delightful, imaginative, and sensory-enticing experience.

Lynn Louise Wonders, MA, LPC, CPCS, RPT-S™
www.WondersCounseling.com

Kurt Oster has woven together a magnificent tapestry of enchantment, courage, and affirmation into Time's mystical journey for self-discovery, revealing the wonder and awe of finding and celebrating one's true self."

Mary L. Affee, Ed.D, LCSW, RPT-S™
Founder/CEO, Horizon Integrated Wellness Group, PLLC
NASW-NC 2023 SOCIAL WORKER OF YEAR
Past President-NC Association For Play Therapy
Certified Synergetic Play Therapist

THIS BOOK BELONGS TO

____

Long ago, when Time was still young, they longed for a place where everyone is accepted, where darkness' shadow has no bearing on them, a place where no one lives in fear or is judged for being truly divergent.

For Time, this place exists only in their imagination.

Then, one day, from sheer boredom, they decided to create that magical place.

Palettes of paint line up like soldiers in perfect order, thin and medium-sized brushes to the left, rough-edged brushes to the right, each standing at attention.

As if it is a game to outdo one another, each brush breathes life into the colors that have faded from disuse.

They create an expansive world within their bristles that Time can see on the canvas but cannot yet reach.

The brushes are laid out like guardsmen who never rest.

The #6 brush, first, standing tall and proud. The #8 brush is confident and full of whimsy. The #10 brush is steadfast and reliable through thick and thin.

Time lays out each of the brushes in perfect order, lined up from tallest to shortest, from softest to most coarse.

Time stands quietly, thinking about reaching for the #4 brush. Then, they stop.

Reaching for the #6 brush, they stop again. They study each brush, picking each one up, and examining it.

"Hmm, which one to choose? They all have good qualities."

"That's it! #8 is just perfect," Time declares excitedly.

The green paint begins dripping from the brush in thick drops onto the floor.

Careful, careful, Time says to themself, their hands shaking from nervousness, for this is a choice that will determine their fate.

Time applies the paint slowly and carefully until, suddenly, the new world magically springs into life.

"Presto."

Time is careful not to get paint everywhere.

They make sure every drop is set just right, knowing all too well how upset they will be if any paint gets spilled, knowing that they would have to start all over again.

The place Time creates is a place that is meant to be perfect.

The place Time creates sits at a magical crossroads, where a choice can be made between fantasy and boredom.

"One must always have a choice," Time shouts as he creates two paths.

"One path leads to the fantasy Arcane world and the other to the boredom of the Mundane world."

When he is done, Time smiles.

The path leading to the Arcane world is hidden from everyone seeking it.

The fantasy world is known for its beauty, wisdom, kindness, and happiness, a place where all are welcome.

It is a place of fun and imagination, something the darkness is not about.

It is a place called the "Time Variance." A place where everyone can be different.

Here, people can do what they want, be what they want to be, act how they wish, hide if they choose, and love how (and who) they want to love.

For you see, Time is divergent, constantly changing, and constantly misunderstood.

Time struggles to make friends. Time is quiet. Time is loud.

Time is organized, but, then again, Time is unorganized.

Time can easily remember things. But then, they can just as easily forget.

Time is time, and they can do anything they choose, even when others believe that they can't.

Curious about this new world but momentarily scared, Time creates a village for visitors to begin their journey.

"It has to be a place where one could stop to rest, but the village must also be filled with wonder and surprise."

The people of the village are kind and wise but also different. Each one is unique.

And because the people of the village are so diverse, they named the main street "Mystical Way" as it is truly a uniquely different street.

As one enters the Mystical Way, one finds a mix of experiences for the senses.

Some parts of the street are gentle and soft on which to walk.

In other parts, the street is firm and rigid.

Some parts of the village are calm, where Arcane can sit quietly to eat and whisper together.

In other parts, the Arcane are loud and boisterous, spilling out into the courtyards to enjoy each other's company.

On your way down the street, a voice calls out to you.

Turning, you see Pierre, the restauranteur, who, oddly, has fashioned their eatery out of an old tree.

He is a quiet man who keeps to himself unless you talk to him about his favorite subject—art.

After hours of discussing styles and features, one might feel inclined to leave, but when Pierre recounts stories of the artifacts he has studied over the years, everyone can feel his warmth and excitement.

The only time that one might spot Pierre outside of the restaurant is in times of need.

If someone is hurt or requires assistance, Pierre is there with his legendary potions.

Pierre is considered to be the village's top potions master. His concoctions are renowned worldwide.

Still, Pierre thinks of them only as "simple potions."

Across the street is a flashy shop filled with bright and vibrant colors, owned by Jewels, the Lady of Stones.

Her shop is filled with stones of every size, shape, and color, and trinkets of every kind, sourced from countries all over the world.

Additionally, she carries exquisitely crafted items, such as gold rings and necklaces made from twisted brass.

People often gather outside Jewels' store, looking at the collection inside with awe until they find something that speaks to them, and they buy it.

Yet, Jewel keeps a sharp eye on her wares.

If someone moves an item out of place, the store will close for several hours before reopening with the items all back in perfect order and in their proper places.

For Jewel, everything has to be perfectly organized.

Further down the street is a shop that defies categorization.

If asked, the villagers would call it the "Shop of Noise."

And if Time had his way, he'd label each entrance with one of his "stop-and-halt" signs, along with complimentary headphones.

Then, anyone passing by and hearing the loud noises coming out of the shop could borrow some headphones and put them on as they walk by.

Clang, bang! Clang, boom! radiates out from the workshop of Ungard, the metal master.

If you bring him any piece of scrap metal, he will give you a full analysis before turning it into something new and unique.

Still, as skilled as he is in creating items from scratch, his shop continuously looks cluttered due to all his projects—some barely started and others nearing completion.

He manages to finish only one endeavor each year.

Once you have visited Ungard's smithery, you must visit Cherry's bakery.

This shop is renowned for its treats that contain mysterious ingredients and attract people from all corners of the land.

The sweets are legendary.

So is Cherry, who is glimpsed only once or twice but is always present somewhere in the shop.

Every morning at 8:13 (not a minute before or a minute after), the bakery opens.

When the door opens, villagers are already waiting in line to buy these remarkable delicacies.

Within thirteen minutes, the shelves with their thirteen cakes are all empty.

13

This is precisely how Cherry wants it.

For Cherry, everything is set according to the number 13.

Down from Cherry's Bakery and across the giant plaza stands the clock tower.

The clock tower rises above the other buildings and keeps a watchful eye on the activities below.

The clock tower houses the shop of Time's younger sister, Citrine.

The villagers are still not sure what to make of Citrine's clock shop, as she is a peculiar character.

Her highly crafted timepieces are made with exquisite materials.

Sometimes, the people of the village are surprised when they retrieve their clocks after Citrine has fixed them.

Because, when they get them back, the timepieces work so well that they can take their owners on magical journeys to faraway lands to see their loved ones.

Citrine's shop is unique in that it boasts a clock for every purpose.

Yet, often, the villagers want something more mundane—ordinary clocks that only tell the time.

Time is perplexed by this preference.

Given that the village is all about uniqueness, Time wonders aloud, "Why would anyone want plain old clocks?"

Then, one day, the vacant shop next to Citrine's clock shop is filled with vibrant books of all types, shapes, and sizes.

Peering through the door, Time can see shelves lined with books.

Some are made of light paper, others of heavy parchment.

Some are large books, and some are pocket-sized.

Some only have words, and others are all pictures.

Children's books share the shelves with other great works of literature, allowing patrons to check out books of any variety from the new library.

But no one came to the new shop.

Biblia, the librarian in charge, felt sad.

"My books are extraordinary, but I must have brought the wrong ones to this town. I wonder why no one is interested in reading them."

As Biblia strolls through the library, a knock on the door resounds like a drum.

Biblia rushes over to open the door and finds Time and his sister, Citrine, holding an enchanted clock.

"Hi! We are your next-door neighbors. We've brought you this clock as a gift," Time says, smiling.

"Oh wow! Thank you very much," Biblia replies, wiping her damp eyes.

The clock begins to tick and wondrously flies around the room, bringing some of the stories within its walls to life.

Each story plays out around them as the villagers, passing on the street, stop and look in the windows in amazement.

"What is wrong?" Citrine asks.

"You are the first visitors to my place. No one else has come in. Everyone is staying away," Biblia replies sadly.

"We are a diverse community. Each of us is unique, and we each take time to come around in our own way to newcomers," explains Citrine.

"But here, on the Mystical Way, you can be who you want to be and do what you want to do," declares Time.

With a nod and a smile, Biblia begins to spin around.

Her hair turns purple, and her robes turn blue and green.

And the library lights up with the colors of the rainbow, catching the eyes of the bystanders.

Minutes later, the people from the village begin coming into the library.

Time chuckles. "See? All one has to do is be themselves!"

"You see, the Mystical Way celebrates diversity, cherishes the individuality of everyone, and emphasizes the world's capacity to transform when one is true to themselves and has pride in all they do."

THE END

or is it?

Definitions

Arcane: known or knowable only to a few people, secret, mysterious, obscure, esoteric, magical, an enigmatic, mystical force in the world, heavenly or spiritual, arcane magic entails forces or phenomena that somehow transcend the natural laws that govern the world by directly manipulating unknown energies that bend the fabric of reality to create a desired effect.

Mundane: of this earthly world, relating to, belonging to, or characteristic of the earth, earthly, in relation to the immediate concerns and activities of human beings.

About the Author

Kurt W. Oster, LICSW, LCSW, MAT, RPT™ is a gay author, clinical social worker, and educator who advocates for the needs of children through his practice as a clinical social worker and as a Registered Play Therapist™.

His writing is devoted to encouraging the transformation of children with attention deficits, autism spectrum disorder, anxiety, OCD, ODD, learning challenges, and coming out issues. He explores these traditionally unspoken topics and brings awareness to neglected groups via his literary works and bibliotherapy that features neurodivergent and LGBTQ characters.

Kurt obtained his Bachelor of Arts (BA) from Rutgers University, a Master's in Social Work (MSW) from the University of Pennsylvania, and Master of Arts in Teaching (MAT) in Elementary Education from the University of Southern California. Through his writing, he aims to demonstrate that anything can be achieved while making storytelling enjoyable and changing how it is done. This is Kurt's fourth book for young adults and his first children's book.

Activity

Imagine a world that exists beyond our own. One where magic is the norm and wonder is an everyday occurrence. You are given the unique opportunity to create the Mystical Way, to build it from the ground up.

Instructions

1. What would your Mystical Way look like? Imagine a place teeming with life and color, where every tree has a personality of its own, and every flower sings its own song. Envision a landscape that is as diverse as it is beautiful, where mountains reach toward the sky, and rivers twist and turn through lush green valleys.

2. Who would live in this wondrous place? Picture beings that are as unique as they are fantastic. Perhaps some fairies float on delicate wings, mischievous sprites lurk behind every bush, or wise old wizards conjure spells with nothing more than a flick of their wrist.

3. What sets your Mystical Way apart from any other? Is it the way the light filters through the leaves of the trees? Or perhaps it's how the stars shine brighter in your magical realm than in ours. Maybe it's something even more unique, like how everyone here sees the world through eyes unburdened by cynicism and doubt.

4. And amid all this wonder, develop a character that expresses your unique identity, someone who embodies all the traits that make you special. Will they be brave, adventurous, kind-hearted, or fiercely independent? It's up to you to decide.

5. So, go forth and create your own Mystical Way, a world of magic, mystery, and limitless possibilities.